Text © 2020 by Lucy Falcone

Illustrations © 2020 by Anna Wilson

Published by POW! a division of powerHouse Packaging & Supply, Inc.

32 Adams Street, Brooklyn, NY 11201-1021

info@powkidsbooks.com
http://powkidsbooks.com
http://powerHouseBooks.com
http://powerHousePackaging.com

Printing and binding by Toppan Leefung

Book design by Robert Avellan

Library of Congress Control Number: 2020945557
ISBN: 978-1-57687-945-0

10 9 8 7 6 5 4 3 2 1

Printed in China

"Dedicated to those who resist with all their might..." —LF

"...and those that inspire and support them." —AW

THE LIBRARIAN'S STORIES

WRITTEN BY
LUCY FALCONE

ILLUSTRATED BY
ANNA WILSON

POW!

Brooklyn, NY

The town I live in is filled with people who are scared—like me.

Our lights are out.
Our water has stopped running.
"Come," Papa says.
Together we carry plastic bottles and
quietly slip outside.

Near the market Papa finds someone selling bread. He tucks a loaf under his coat.

Then we fill our bottles with water from a pipe.

Mama smiles as she cuts the bread into three pieces, and we eat.

The next morning Papa and I pass crumbling buildings.

They look like ghosts.

The line for water is long, but I am
happy to meet a friend from school.

As Papa and I walk
home, we hear words.

The words grow louder.
They come from the square
in front of our apartment.

It's the librarian.

Papa shakes his head. "Foolish woman," he says, but he stays to listen.

We don't have much food to eat today.

Mama stops me from watering the
small plant on our kitchen table.

In the morning, gray light pours through the window. I crawl out from under my blanket and move the curtain aside.

I see my cousin, Anna, standing in a doorway like a statue.

Everything looks frozen—except the librarian.

I close my eyes.
Her words carry me back…

...to my birthday.
Before everything
changed.

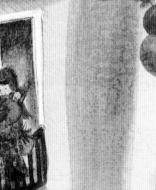

I have a different wish now.

Mama worries when I'm at the window too long. She gently pulls me away. "Too dangerous," she says.

Sorry for you

The next day Anna, Tarik,
and I listen from the stairs.

The librarian's stories
make us laugh.

They help us
remember

...what life

was like before.

Tanks move through
our square.
We hide when we
see them.

The town I live in is filled with people who are scared—like me.

glade of silver birch trees there was no trac... they are

Every day the librarian comes.
Every day she sits on the
bench and reads.

Soldiers march through
our town today.

We don't make a sound until
long after the marching stops.

Will the librarian come?

I wait... ...and wait.

As the sun goes down I hear words...

...and I rush to look.

Mama and Papa wrap their arms around me. We listen together.

Time has passed and the
soldiers are gone.

People have come
back to our square.

Everyone works together
to clean up the rubble.

I want to help.

The town I live in is
filled with hope.

"Darkness cannot drive
out darkness;
only light can do that."

— MARTIN LUTHER KING, Jr.—

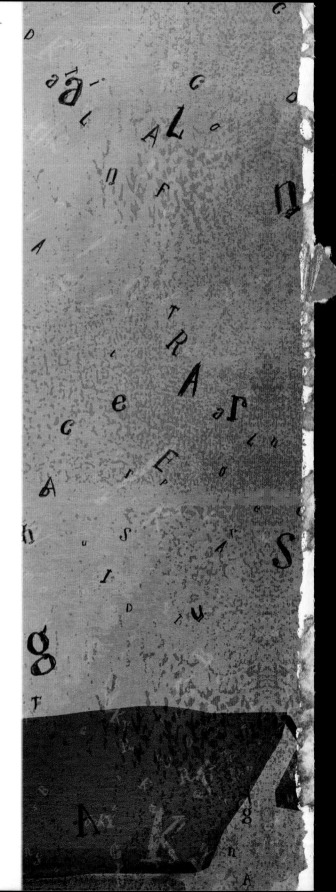

THE LIBRARIAN'S STORIES

I was inspired to write *The Librarian's Stories* after reading *The Cellist of Sarajevo*, a book based on the true story of a musician who played his cello for 22 days to mark the deaths of 22 innocent people killed after the bombing of a bakery during the Bosnian war.

As a writer, I believe in the power of stories to keep hope alive, to bring healing and light in the darkest of times. And who better to bring stories to families traumatized by war than a courageous librarian.

***

A second theme in *The Librarian's Stories* is the burning of libraries. Over centuries, thousands of them have been destroyed. One in particular stood out for me. During the Islamic Golden Age in the 13th century, an invading Mongol army set fire to all the libraries in Baghdad, and the books from the House of Wisdom were thrown into the Tigris River. There were so many of them that they created a bridge for the Mongol army to cross. Legend says that the pages bled ink into the river for seven days, draining them of their knowledge. When the books stopped bleeding, the courageous people of Bagdad started rebuilding their city.

Millions of books have been burned in the senseless violence of war. Many rulers in the past, and the present, feel threatened by stories and ideas and knowledge. They know that books can change people. They know that books can change the world. To them, this is dangerous. They don't want people to learn, to understand, to think for themselves. They don't want people to remember their history.

LUCY FALCONE is a former children's television writer for such series as *The Littlest Hobo* and Nickelodeon's hugely popular, *Are You Afraid of the Dark?* She turned her hand to writing a number of award-winning novels and a junior-fiction detective series. Her debut picture book, *I Didn't Stand Up*, won the 2019 Elementary Teachers Federation of Ontario Children's Literature Award. *The Librarian's Stories* is her second, emotionally resonant, picture book.

ANNA WILSON is a freelance designer and illustrator who has spent most of her adult life travelling the world. She loves storms and snow and is happiest running in the mountains or drawing in the streets of new cities. This is her first picture book.